To my sister Wendy.

Thank you Jesus, my Lord and Savior.

DIAL BOOKS FOR YOUNG READERS • A divison of Penguin Young Readers Group. • Published by The Penguin Group •
Penguin Group (USA) Inc., 375 Hudson Street, New York, NY 10014, U.S.A. • Penguin Group (Canada), 10 Alcorn Avenue,
Toronto, Ontario, Canada M4V 3B2 (a division of Pearson Penguin Canada Inc.) • Penguin Books Ltd, 80 Strand,
London WC2R 0RL, England • Penguin Ireland, 25 St. Stephen's Green, Dublin 2, Ireland (a division of Penguin Books Ltd) •
Penguin Books India Pvt Ltd, 11 Community Centre, Panchsheel Park, New Delhi-110 017, India • Penguin Group (NZ),
Cnr Airborne and Rosedale Roads, Albany, Auckland, New Zealand (a division of Pearson New Zealand Ltd) • Penguin
Books (South Africa) (Pty) Ltd, 24 Sturdee Avenue, Rosebank, Johannesburg 2196, South Africa •
Penguin Books Ltd, Registered Offices: 80 Strand, London WC2R 0RL, England

1 3 5 7 9 10 8 6 4 2

Copyright © 2005 by Kevin Luthardt • All rights reserved
Manufactured in China on acid-free paper • Set in Bookman • Designed by Teresa Kietlinski
LIBRARY OF CONGRESS CATALOGING-IN-PUBLICATION DATA • Luthardt, Kevin.• You're weird! / Kevin Luthardt.
p.   cm.   SUMMARY: Rabbit and Turtle each make fun of the other's peculiarities, but they turn out to have
some things in common after all.
ISBN 0-8037-2986-3 [1. Behavior—Fiction. 2. Rabbits—Fiction. 3. Turtles—Fiction.] I. Title.
PZ7.L9793Yo 2005   [E]—dc22   2004006042
The art was created using watercolors on paper.

9.99 8/05
Ingram
32984

YOU'RE WEiRD!

Kevin Luthardt

Dial Books for Young Reader New York

Whatcha doin'?

I'm playing with my trucks.
Do you want to play with me?

No thanks.

My airplanes are way better.

Let's play the drums!

No way! I play the saxophone!

Well, how about baseball?
Everyone likes baseball.

Nah.
I only play football.

Vanilla
ice cream?

Chocolate!

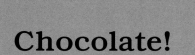

WEIRD!
WEIRD!
WEIRD!

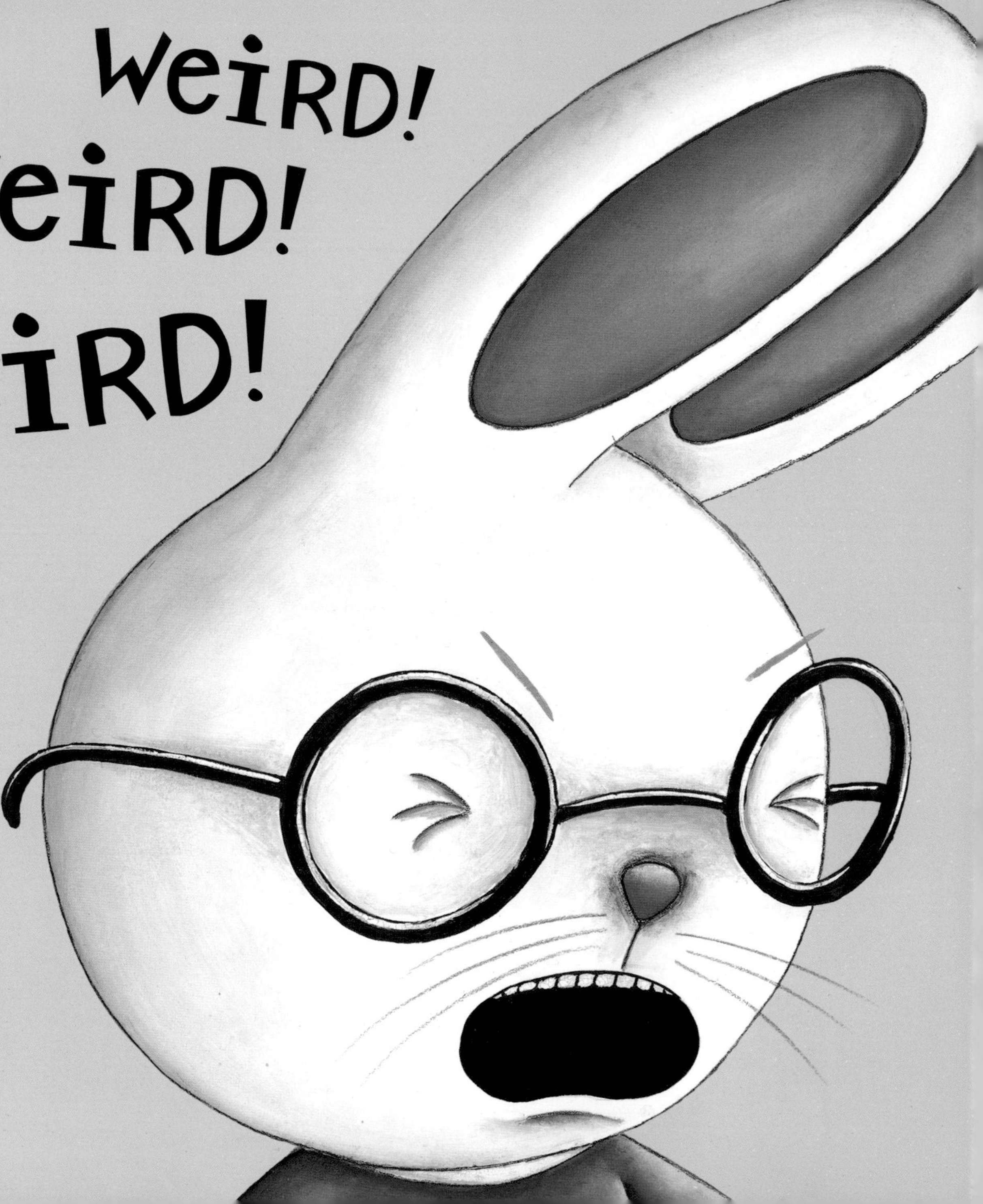

Cool! And I like cotton candy . . .

with
ketchup
AND
mustard!

Yum! How about watermelon . . .

with peanut butter?